Brown Bear,

Copyright © 1967, 1983 by Holt, Rinehart and Winston
All rights reserved, including the right to reproduce this
book or portions thereof in any form.
Published by Holt, Rinehart and Winston,
383 Madison Avenue, New York, New York 10017.
Published simultaneously in Canada by Holt, Rinehart and
Winston of Canada, Limited.

Library of Congress Cataloging in Publication Data

Martin, Bill, 1916–
   Brown bear, Brown bear, what do you see?

   Summary: Children see a variety of animals, each one
a different color, and a mother looking at them.
   [1. Color—Fiction. 2. Animals—Fiction. 3. Stories
in rhyme] I. Carle, Eric, ill. II. Title.
PZ8.3.M418Br 1983   [E]   83-12779
ISBN 0-03-064164-0

First published in 1967 in a slightly different form by the School Division,
Holt, Rinehart and Winston.
First General Book edition—1983

Printed in the United States of America
10 9 8 7 6 5 4 3

Brown Bear,
What Do You See?

by Bill Martin, Jr.
Pictures by Eric Carle

Holt, Rinehart and Winston · New York

"Brown Bear,
Brown Bear,
What do you see?"

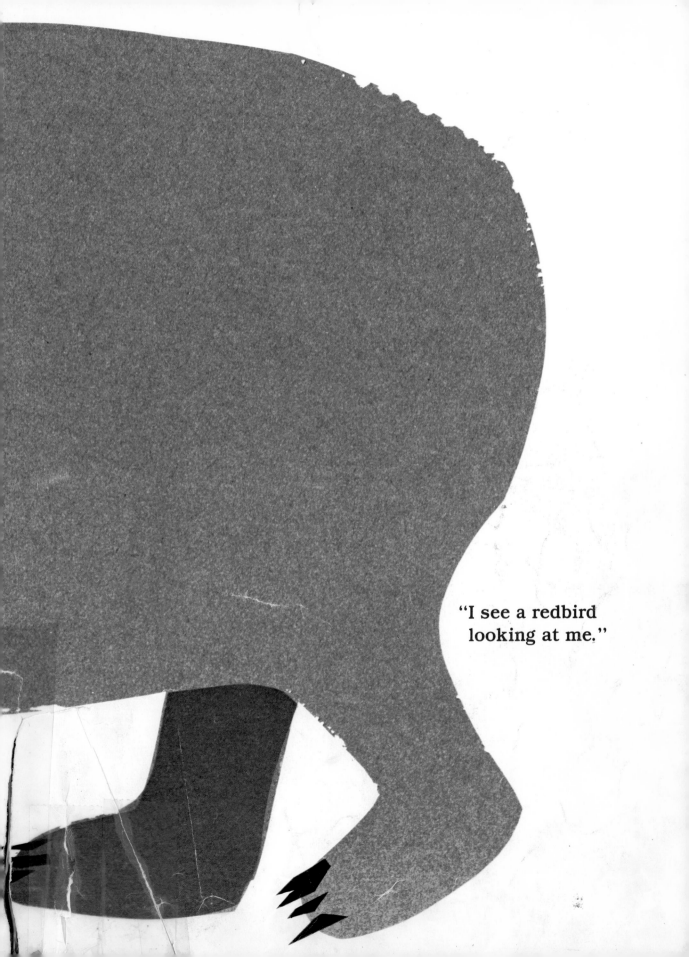

"I see a redbird
looking at me."

"Redbird,
redbird,
What do you see?"

"I see a yellow duck
looking at me."

"Yellow duck,
yellow duck,
What do you see?"

"I see a blue horse
looking at me."

"Blue horse,
 blue horse,
 What do you see?"

"I see a green frog
looking at me."

"Green frog,
 green frog,
 What do you see?"

"I see a purple cat
looking at me."

"Purple cat,
 purple cat,
What do you see?"

"I see a white dog
looking at me."

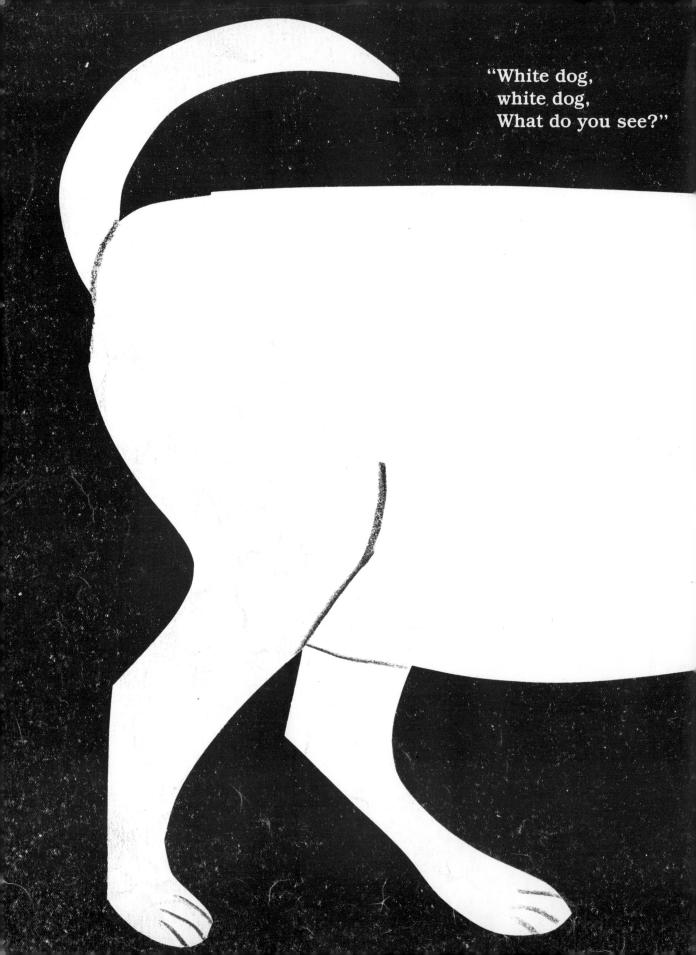

"White dog,
white dog,
What do you see?"

"I see a black sheep
looking at me."

"Black sheep,
black sheep,
What do you see?"

"I see a goldfish
looking at me."

"Goldfish,
 goldfish,
 What do you see?"

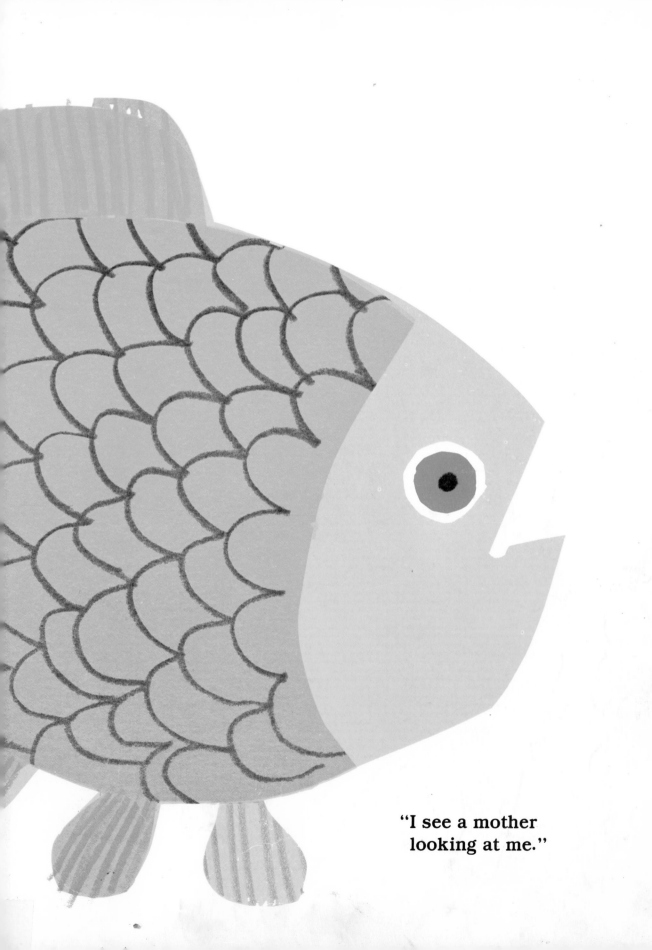

"I see a mother
looking at me."

"Mother,
   mother,
 What do you see?"

"I see beautiful children
looking at me."

"Children
children,
What do you see?"

"We see a brown bear,   a redbird,

a green frog,

a black sheep,   a goldfish,

a yellow duck,

a blue horse,

a purple cat,

a white dog,

and a mother looking at us.
That's what we see."